The Homework Caper

by JOAN M. LEXAU
Pictures by SYD HOFF

An I Can

A Harper

Harper & Row, Publishers

I Can Read Book is a registered trademark of
Harper & Row, Publishers, Inc.
The Homework Caper
Text copyright © 1966 by Joan M. Lexau
Illustrations copyright © 1966 by Syd Hoff
For information address Harper & Row Junior Books, 10 East 53rd
Street, New York, N.Y. 10022. Published simultaneously in
Canada by Fitzhenry & Whiteside Limited, Toronto.
Library of Congress Catalog Card Number: 66-11493
Trade ISBN 0-06-023855-0
Harpercrest ISBN 0-06-023856-9
Trophy ISBN 0-06-444088-5
First Harper Trophy edition, 1985.

For John

It was five after nine

on a Tuesday in May.

Miss Green said,

"Pass up your homework."

Ken Noonan took a paper

out of his arithmetic book.

He passed it to his friend Bill.

Bill took a paper

out of his arithmetic book.

He said, "Hey, this isn't mine.

Where did this come from?

Where is my homework?"

He looked again in his book.

His homework wasn't in it.

Miss Green came to his desk.

"What is it, Bill?" she asked.

"I can't find my homework.

Just this funny paper," Bill said.

Ken got up from his desk

and looked at the paper.

It had numbers all over it.

Funny-looking numbers.

It was not a homework paper.

"I did my homework," Bill said.

"I put it in my book, just like always."

Ken looked in Bill's book.

He even looked in his own book.

They looked around on the floor.

Bill's homework was gone.

Miss Green said, "It's all right, Bill.

I know you always do your homework.

After school, try to find your paper."

Ken and Bill were good friends.

Ken wanted to help Bill.

He thought and thought about it.

At last he thought of a way to help.

"Well, Ken?" Miss Green said.

"Huh?" said Ken.

"I asked if you would like

to read out loud now," she said.

"Oh. No, thank you," Ken said

before he thought. "I mean, yes."

Bill had to show him where to read.

After school Ken told Bill,

"This is what we'll do.

You do everything you did yesterday.

I will watch you. We will see

what could have happened

to your homework."

"What did I do yesterday?" Bill said.

"Well, I ate breakfast at your place.

No, that was this morning."

"Anyway, I mean after school," Ken said.

"Let's see," Bill said. "We went home.

We got out of our school clothes.

And we played ball."

"So let's do the same things today,"

Ken said.

They went home.

Ken went into his building.

Bill went into the building next door.

They got out of their school clothes.

Ken looked out of his window

at Bill's window.

"It couldn't happen yet," Ken yelled.

"You haven't done your homework yet."

Bill yelled back,

"You ate here yesterday.

My mother said you can eat here again."

"Good," Ken said. "I'll tell my mother.

See you downstairs."

Ken looked for his ball.

He couldn't find it.

"Mother, where's my ball,
and may I eat at Bill's?" he called.

"I don't know,
and you ate there last night,"
his mother said.

"Bill asked me," Ken said.

"His mother knows I'm coming."

"Well, all right," his mother said.

"I know where your ball is,"
said his little sister, Susan.
"Where?" Ken asked her.
"In my hand," Susan said.
Ken got mad.

"Look," he yelled,

"you keep your hands off my things.

How many times do I have to tell you?"

"It was under your bed.

I found it for you," Susan said.

She threw it under the bed again.

"Well, why didn't you say so?" said Ken.

Ken went downstairs.

Bill was there.

Before they could cross the street,

Susan came downstairs.

"Can I play?" she said.

"Can I? Can I? Can I?"

"No, you can't," Ken said.

"Yes, I can," Susan said.

Ken told her,

"You can't cross the street alone,

and I'm not going to cross you.

Some other time

you can play with me."

"You always say that," Susan said.

"You're mean." She started to cry.

Ken felt bad about it.

But he didn't want

to play ball with Susan.

21

He crossed the street with Bill.

They were playing catch

when they saw Susan watching them.

"How did you get here?" Ken asked.

"A big girl crossed me," Susan said.

"Well, go play with her then," said Ken.

He looked at the girl.

"Thanks a *lot*," he said.

"That's okay," she said.

Susan said to Ken,

"But I want to watch you."

Ken told her,

"Well, as long as you're here,

you can get the balls I miss.

But after this, don't come after me

all the time."

They were still playing ball
when Bill's mother called to them
from the window.
"Time to eat," she said.

After Ken took Susan to his building,

he went to Bill's to eat.

After they ate, Ken said,

"Yesterday I did my homework at home.

But today I will do it here.

I will see what happens

to your homework."

"Good idea," Bill said.

"Do you think you can get

my homework from yesterday back?"

"We'll see if my idea works," said Ken.

Ken went home and got his book
and came back. They sat down
and began working.

Bill's big brother came in

to do his homework.

It was quiet.

There was little talking.

When they were done,

Ken said, "It's quiet here.

At home Susan is always saying,

'What are you doing?

I want to do it too.'"

Bill's brother said,

"Bill used to be like that too

when he was little.

He had to do everything I did."

"Who, me?" Bill said.

"I don't remember that."

"I remember it," his brother said.

"It was before you went to school.

Then I got an idea.

I gave you homework to do.

I told you to draw pictures.

I showed you how to make words.

"Then you were quiet
and I could do my homework."
Bill said, "I must have been crazy,
wanting to do homework
when I didn't have to."

31

Ken's mother called to him
from his window.

"Coming," Ken called back.

Ken said to Bill,

"I didn't find out yet
about your homework.

But I will think about it some more.

Before you go to bed,
make sure you have *this* homework.

Come over for breakfast.

We will talk about it then."

As he went out the door

he dropped his book.

Two papers fell out.

He picked them up. He said,

"Here's the homework I just did.

But what's this other paper?"

"Hey, that's the homework

I did yesterday," Bill said.

"You had it all the time.

I don't think that's very funny, Ken."

"But I didn't have it.

"I even looked in my book for it.

Don't you remember?" Ken said.

"Then how come it's in your book?"

asked Bill.

Ken didn't know.

"This is crazy," he said.

"But I'll find out what happened

somehow. See you in the morning."

Bill didn't say anything.

Ken went home. He felt bad.

When he got home, Susan said,

"Tell me a story."

"Some other time," Ken said.

"I have to think right now."

"You're mean," Susan yelled.

"Mean, mean, mean, mean!"

"Susan, it's time for bed,"
her mother said.
"I will read you a story
when you are in bed."

Susan went to her room

and shut the door with a bang.

39

"That kid is always after me,"
Ken said.

"I know," his mother said.

"But you're her big brother.
She looks up to you.
You used to play with her a lot.
Now you almost never do.
How would you feel
if you were Susan?"

"Okay," Ken said.

"I'll tell her a story."

Ken made up a story
about a tired old dragon.
Susan fell asleep before the end.
Ken had to go on telling the story
to himself to find out what happened.

After he went to bed,

Ken thought about Bill's homework.

He didn't get any new ideas.

"I hope Bill comes for breakfast.

I hope he doesn't stay mad," he thought.

In the morning, Bill didn't come.

Ken called out the window,

"Hey, Bill, aren't you coming?"

"Be right there," Bill said.

When Bill came over, Ken asked,

"Why didn't you come sooner?

I thought you were still mad."

"No, I wasn't mad," Bill told him.

"I thought about it, and I knew

you wouldn't take my homework

and not tell me all day.

But I thought maybe *you* got mad

because I thought you took it."

"I'm not mad," Ken said.

"Do you still have your new homework?

Bill looked in his book.

"Yes, it's still here," he said.

"And my old homework too."

"I sure don't know what happened
to your homework yesterday," Ken said.

"I just don't know."

"What will I tell the teacher?" Bill asked.

"Tell her you don't know what happened,"

Ken said. "That's all you can tell her.

Anyway you have the homework now."

After breakfast

they started out for school.

Susan started out after them.

"I'm going to school too," she said.

"No, you stay home with me,"
her mother told her.
"Later, we will play school.
I will show you
how to make some more numbers."
Ken said to Bill, "Let's get going
before Susan starts to bawl."

They went down the stairs.

Ken stopped.

Bill bumped into him.

"Hey! Numbers!" Ken said.

He ran up the stairs.

Bill ran after him.

Ken said, "Susan, did you put
a paper with numbers on it
in Bill's book when he was
here for breakfast yesterday?

"And did you take his paper

out of his book?"

"No, I didn't," Susan said.

"Oh," said her brother.

"Well, it was just an idea.

Come on, Bill, let's go."

"It was *your* book," Susan said.

"I took your homework

and gave you my homework.

You yelled at me

when I found your ball.

So I put your homework back.

I didn't want it anymore."

"Our books look the same," said Ken.

"That was an awful thing

you did to Bill, Susan.

It's good the teacher wasn't mad.

But it was an awful thing to do."

Susan started to cry.

"But I gave you *my* homework," she said.

"It isn't the same thing," Ken told her.

"It isn't?" she said.

"No," said Ken. "Not at all.

The teacher doesn't want your homework."

Bill said, "She didn't mean

to do anything bad.

Did you, Susan?"

"No," Susan bawled.

"It was a present for Ken."

"Some present!" Ken said.

"You must never do that again.

"But if you stop your bawling,

I'll tell you what I'll do.

When I do my homework today,

I will give you homework to do.

Bill's brother used to do it.

How would you like that?"

Susan stopped crying.

"I'd like that," she said.

She waved when Ken and Bill

went downstairs again.

They waved back to her.

At school Bill told Miss Green,

"I have my homework from yesterday.

That funny paper was a present.

A present from Ken's little sister."

Miss Green laughed. "A present!
That's a new one," she said.
"I never would have thought of that."
"Well, I'm glad Ken figured it out,"
Bill said.

Ken said, "I thought

if you did the same things again,

I could figure it out.

And my idea worked, that's all."

"It sure did," said Bill.

"Thanks a lot."

"Oh, anytime," Ken said, "anytime."